nickelodeon™

VICTORIOUS™

nickelodeon™

VICTORIOUS™

The New Girl

Adapted by
Xanna Eve Chown

Based on
"Victorious" and
"The Bird Scene,"
written by Dan Schneider

Victorious TV series
created by Dan Schneider

Random House 🏠 New York

Chapter One

Introducing Tori

Stinky fish mold or singing practice—
which would YOU choose?

Sixteen-year-old Tori Vega was standing in her parents' spacious kitchen in Los Angeles. Her study buddy Evan was hunched over his laptop. Tori's life was about to change forever. But she didn't have a clue about that yet. At the moment she was only concerned with a piece of moldy bread that was hanging in front of her nose.

Evan and Tori were working on their school science project: a mold bush. Two weeks earlier, they had stuck twigs into a plant pot and used binder clips to attach a piece of food to each one. The mold had grown on the twigs in odd shapes.

It would have looked kind of artistic if it hadn't been so gross! Today, Tori's job was to describe the different kinds of mold while Evan took notes.

Tori put down the folder she was holding and reached for a magnifying glass.

"The bread mold," she began, flicking back her long brown hair with a sigh. As usual, she was dressed cute and casual in a denim skirt with sandals, a gray T-shirt, and a purple hoodie.

"The bread mold," Evan repeated, enthusiastically, typing the words into his laptop.

"Furry," said Tori. She reached out and touched it. Yuck. It was hard to share Evan's enthusiasm. "Mushy," she continued. They had to record the look, feel, and smell of the different molds. During what part of her future life would this be useful? Sometimes homework was a mystery to Tori.

"Next, the fish mold," she said as she leaned forward, touched the mold gingerly, and inhaled. "Stinky," she said, wishing she hadn't taken such a big sniff.

Tori was about to move on to the next batch of mold, when *BANG!* she was saved by the noise of

the front door flying open. It was her older sister, Trina, dramatic as ever.

"I am *so* upset!" she shouted. Trina was never one to hide her feelings. If anything, she made all her emotions big. Huge. Gargantuan!

"You won't believe who I got partnered with for the Big Showcase!" she said, marching into the living room in her high heels. She threw her bag and keys on the sofa and faced the two lab partners with their science experiment. "Andrew Harris . . . a *tenth* grader." She growled the words "tenth grader" as if she were saying "complete idiot."

Tori frowned. She and Evan were in the tenth grade. And Trina was only a year older.

"What's the Big Showcase?" asked Evan.

"It's a performance they put on at her school every year," explained Tori. Tori and Trina went to different schools. And Trina's wasn't just different—it was *different*.

Trina loved to sing, dance, act, and be the center of attention. That was why she fit in so well at Hollywood Arts, a high school that only admitted L.A.'s most creative, talented kids. Tori went to Sherwood High, which was just a typical school.

She liked it, even though the homework included sniffing different types of mold.

Tori glanced over at her science project. She was done with Trina's drama and was ready to get back to work. Trina, however, was just getting started.

Trina took Evan's hand and led him across the room as she spoke. "They invite agents and directors and producers and other super-powerful people in show business and it's extremely important to me," said Trina as she approached the front door. "Which is why I am very upset. And goodbye!" She pushed Tori's friend out the door and slammed it shut, not even pausing when Evan began to complain. Poor Evan. He had no idea that when the steam train Trina came to town, it was best to just get out of the way.

"Hey!" yelled Tori. "He and I have a science project due tomorrow. I have to turn in my mold bush!"

Tori was used to Trina's "me first" outlook on life, but this was too much!

"No!" Trina said, crossing the living room. "Andrew's coming over and you've got to help us

4

figure out what we're going to do in the Big Showcase! I definitely want to sing!" She approached the piano, played a chord, threw back her head, and sang: "Nyahhhh!"

The sound was like the combination of a car horn and a sick goose.

"How was that?" she asked.

"Loud," Tori replied truthfully.

"Awesome," said Trina, looking very pleased with herself.

Tori grinned. Trina was just . . . Trina. Even when she drove Tori crazy, she still managed to make her little sister smile.

The doorbell rang.

"Ugh, he's here," said Trina.

Tori went for the door. It was the least she could do. The situation was obviously upsetting Trina.

"Stay!" Trina snapped, as if talking to a dog.

Whatever, thought Tori.

Trina opened the door to reveal a cute guy with a friendly smile on his face.

"Come in," Trina sighed. She was already so over this. She could handle whatever showbiz dealt

her, but working with a tenth grader? Come on!

"Thanks?" the guy said, his friendliness turning to bewilderment.

"Tori, that's Andrew." Trina was already walking away.

"Andre," he corrected her. He turned his smile up to full beam again for Tori. "You go to Hollywood Arts too?"

"Oh no, I'm not a performer! Just my sister," said Tori.

"Yep, I got the talent," Trina explained, "and she got the strong teeth." She grabbed Tori's jaw and squished her face. "You know she's never had one cavity?" Trina continued, releasing Tori from her grip.

"I try not to brag about it," joked Tori, just relieved to have her face back to normal.

Andre grinned. He was obviously amused by the sisters. Then he saw the piano in the corner of the room.

"Wow, nice piano," he cooed.

He sat down and immediately started to play. His fingers glided over the keys, delivering a pretty classical number, finishing with a bluesy, jazzy

flourish. It seemed to take no effort at all. Tori was impressed.

"You're fantastic!" she said.

"He's okay," said Trina.

Andre stopped playing. He frowned and sniffed the air. Then he took Tori's hand, smelled it, and shot her a confused look.

"Fish mold," said Tori.

Andre let go of Tori's hand. It dropped to the piano, making the keys clang. They both laughed. *He's nice,* thought Tori. She was glad her sister had been partnered with Andre. Even if Trina wasn't!

Chapter Two

Practice Makes Perfect

5 DAYS helping Trina and Andre rehearse.
Trina's driving me INSANE!

Andre had been at Tori and Trina's house every day for five days, rehearsing for the Big Showcase. He was so enthusiastic about the upcoming performance that Tori was getting excited too. It was going to be amazing, Andre told her. There would be backup singers and dancers, and his band would be playing onstage with him. All he needed to do now was make sure Trina was ready to perform. But that was going to take some time. . . .

Tori and Andre had become friends, which was good because Tori wasn't allowed to leave her sister's side during rehearsals. Tori had clapped

and critiqued and made herself useful for so long that she knew the song as well as Trina did.

One sunny day, Andre and Tori were taking a break from rehearsal in the garden. Tori's patio had two green sun loungers and an awesome view over the Hollywood Hills. But Andre wasn't relaxing in a chair, and he wasn't admiring the view either. He was pacing up and down the garden, talking on his cell phone. It didn't sound like the conversation was going his way.

"Grandma, listen!" Andre shouted. "There's no way you can drown at my school." He rolled his eyes and Tori chuckled. "You are not going to fall in a toilet! Look, I've got to go. I'll call you later!"

"Your grandmother's coming to the Big Showcase?" Tori asked, sipping her lemonade.

"Yeah," said Andre. "It's going to be the first time she's left the house in six years."

"Six years? Why?" Tori was intrigued.

"The woman's afraid of everything," he explained. "People, umbrellas, rabbis, bikinis, breakfast food . . ."

Tori grinned. She got the picture. "So if she saw a rabbi in a bikini eating pancakes . . ."

"The woman would burst into flames!" finished Andre. Tori knew he was exaggerating, but by the sound of it, not by much.

TWANG! Inside, Trina banged a chord on the piano.

"You guys! Come on!" she screamed.

"Back to rehearsal," said Tori, grabbing her drink and heading for the door.

They entered the house. Wow! Trina had changed her outfit while they were outside. She was wearing a frilly blue and white tiered dress with black ankle boots and a sparkly tiara.

Tori gulped. Her sister looked like a human piñata.

"So, what do you think?" Trina asked her sister. "Fabulous, right?"

"You really need to wear that just to rehearse?" Tori asked.

"A performer needs to feel the part to be the part," said Trina, slowly tapping Tori on the nose with her finger.

"I thought we talked about you not tapping my nose anymore," Tori said in a voice that revealed just how much nose tapping she had to deal with. But as usual, her big sister merely laughed.

"Okay, we got the comedy stuff down, so let's start with my song."

Comedy stuff? thought Tori. *I wasn't joking about the nose tapping!* But there was no point repeating herself now. She'd just have to remind Trina the next time she tapped her nose!

"By *your song,* I'm guessing you mean the song that *I* wrote?" Andre asked.

"No one cares who wrote the song," said Trina. "Now . . ." She paused to clear her throat. "Take it from 'when I make it shine.'"

Andre had only been playing for a few seconds when Trina barked, "Slower!"

So Andre began to play his melody slow and sweet. Then Trina belted out the chorus. She was off-key, off-tempo, off-everything!

When she finished, she smugly looked at the tenth graders and asked, "Well?" She was only being polite. She clearly thought she'd nailed it!

Andre turned to Tori. "Do you have any aspirin?" he asked.

Tori already had a large bottle ready. She popped the cap and offered him a couple.

11

Ditching school—
going to Trina's BIG SHOWCASE

It was the day of the Big Showcase and Tori had skipped school so she could be there. She couldn't miss Trina's performance—not after everything they had been through! Their parents had taken time off work and were sitting proudly beside Tori in the packed auditorium.

Tori was having a great time. The show was really good because the students were so talented. There were comedians, singers, dancers—even jugglers! Tori sat back in her seat and relaxed. It was almost time for her sister's performance. On-stage, two guys were break-dancing, flipping and spinning with the bumping beats. Then she heard a noise from the row behind her. An old lady had arrived late and was pushing past the other people in their seats. They tried to move out of her way, but she twitched, her eyes nervously darting around the room. She was absolutely terrified. She glanced left and right as she took the seat behind Tori, clutching her handbag to her knees. Tori could guess who this was.

"Hi," she whispered. "Are you Andre's grandmother?" She was trying to be friendly, but the old lady squealed in alarm.

"I don't know you!" she screamed, ducking down out of sight. She peeped out from behind the chair. Tori turned back and exchanged confused looks with her parents. Andre's grandma really was scared of everything!

Suddenly, over the noise of the dance music, Tori heard a strange sort of gargling scream. It sounded oddly familiar. The audience shifted uneasily, hoping it would stop. But it came again, louder. The dancers onstage sneaked glances into the wings. There was something going on—a scuffle behind the curtains was distracting them from their routine.

A man in a brown shirt squeezed along Tori's row and gestured wildly to get her parents' attention. It was Lane, Hollywood Arts's guidance counselor.

"Excuse me. Are you Trina's parents?" he asked. He was trying to keep quiet, but everyone was staring.

"Yes, why?" asked Tori's dad uncomfortably.

"Please come with me," Lane said. Tori's parents got up, alarmed, mumbling apologies to the people sitting beside them. Tori followed, hoping Trina was okay. What had happened?

Lane led them backstage, then took them to the wings. They walked past guitars, amps, keyboards, and soundboards. There were big lights, props, and ladders to dodge before they got to Trina. She was wearing her flouncy blue dress and tiara, and was surrounded by a group of students and teachers trying to calm her down. Right beside her was the school nurse, wearing blue latex gloves and holding a tongue depressor. She looked really worried. . . .

Chapter Four

Tongue Troubles

*Not all herbs
are good for you!*

Tori and her parents pushed their way through the throng and stared at Trina in disbelief. Her tongue had swelled to about four times its normal size and was sticking out of her mouth like a pink balloon. Trina was waving her arms around, frantically trying to talk.

"Unthins ong ith ah ang!" she shouted. Tori was pretty sure she was saying "something's wrong with my tongue," but it was hard to tell because, well, something was wrong with her tongue.

"Oh my god, it's huge!" said Tori. She couldn't believe what she was seeing.

"Does anybody know how this happened?" the nurse demanded. It was clear she had never seen anything quite like this before.

Tori thought hard. What had her sister done? Then she remembered she had seen Trina doing something in the kitchen the night before. Something that was supposed to help, not ruin, Trina's performance. "Chinese herb gargle!" Tori blurted out.

Trina frantically nodded and touched her nose like in a game of charades.

"What are you talking about?" asked Mr. Vega.

"Trina found a website that shows you how to make an herb gargle to help you sing better," said Tori. She hadn't thought it sounded like a good idea at the time, but she hadn't known it would be this dangerous either.

"She must have had an allergic reaction to it," said the nurse.

"Ah owth eels ooog!" squealed Trina.

"Will she be okay?" asked her mom, watching in horror as the nurse squeezed Trina's massive tongue.

"Well, her tongue is engorged and—oh gosh,

well, now it's throbbing erratically," said the nurse.

"Throbbing erratically?" Tori repeated.

Finding it hard to keep quiet despite her overgrown tongue, Trina kept trying to speak. But no one could understand a word she said.

"Any way she will be able to perform today?" asked Lane.

"Of course not," scolded the nurse.

Trina threw herself at the nurse, grabbing her collar, trying to speak. Fat tongue or not, she wanted to get on that stage!

"Stop talking!" said the nurse angrily. "Your tongue could burst!"

"Busth?" Trina said, then finally quieted down. This was getting seriously freaky. She looked like she had a full bar of soap shoved in her mouth.

"I'm sorry, sweetie," said their mom.

"Next year," said their dad, rubbing Trina's shoulders.

"I'm going to take her over there," said the nurse firmly. She pulled Trina aside. "And massage her tongue."

Massage her tongue?

The nurse took Trina gently by the arm and led her away to a quiet corner. Mr. and Mrs. Vega followed them. That was when Tori noticed Andre standing nearby. She realized that it wasn't just Trina who would miss out. Andre couldn't perform his song without a singer. And there was his band, and the backup dancers, who had been practicing too.

"I guess my grandma came here for nothing," Andre said sadly.

"Wait," said Lane. "Does anyone else know Trina's part?"

"Her sister does!" said Andre, his face lighting up. He turned to Tori, begging her with his eyes. Tori did not like the way this was going. Not one little bit.

"*Me* sister?" she yelped. "No. I just helped them rehearse! I'm not even a student here." She backed away, holding out her hands to stop anyone from getting closer. But Andre grabbed her and pulled her to one side.

"You know the whole thing inside and out!" said Andre. "The song, the choreography—you can do this!"

"No way," said Tori firmly.

"She said she'll do it!" Andre announced loudly. He flung his arms in the air, and all the students and teachers cheered.

"No, I didn't," said Tori, but her voice was lost in the noise.

"Wait a minute. She can't go onstage . . . ," said Lane. Tori felt relieved. This man would stop the madness. He would understand that she wasn't a performer! ". . . wearing *that,*" he finished.

"Excuse me?" shrieked Tori. She was wearing one of her favorite tops!

"Go and get her something cool to wear," Lane told Andre. Tori looked down at her outfit in disbelief. She started to protest more, but Andre pulled her away to the dressing rooms. The other kids ran after them, whooping and yelling. Everyone loves a makeover!

Tori escaped Andre and ran back, coming to a halt when she reached the stage. She was trapped! She grabbed hold of the back of a chair. The student sitting there continued to drum his drumsticks even when Andre appeared, picked up Tori's legs, and dragged her, along with the chair and the drummer still sitting on it, toward the middle of the room. With her hand holding the chair and Andre pulling at her legs, Tori was completely stretched out.

Her fingers were quickly losing their grip on the chair, and she finally let go. Andre caught her.

"Don't make me do this!" he said, picking her up and carrying her, kicking and screaming, back to the dressing room.

Chapter Five

In the Spotlight

All eyes are on me. . . .
HELP!

The audience waited impatiently. Many were on the phone or in the middle of conversations.

Andre's band was onstage tuning up. Andre walked out and headed to his keyboard. Cries of "Hey, Andre!" suddenly rang through the room. Apparently, he was a very popular guy. The lights lowered and the audience grew quiet, waiting. It was as if they could sense that something special was about to happen. Tori's mom and dad were standing in the wings, watching nervously. The stage looked incredible. The crew had wheeled a wide set of steps to the back, ready for the

dance routine that Tori knew so well.

A hush fell over the crowd. Just then, a muffled squeaking could be heard. It was Tori still trying to get out of performing. "Let go of me! What are you doing? No, please, no!" She was terrified. With a gentle shove, Lane tried to push Tori out onto the top step. She squirmed back toward the wings, but he pushed her up the steps once again. The spotlight operator saw this and swung his light around, bathing her in a white glow. Tori's parents gasped. Their daughter was barely recognizable in a sparkling minidress and pink and silver sneakers.

This was it. She was onstage and couldn't fight anymore. The lights were blinding her. She couldn't make out the faces in the audience. In a funny way, this helped. She could see Andre sitting at his keyboard. He gave her a reassuring smile, then nodded to his band, as if to say "Here we go." Then they started to play the introduction to Andre's song.

From the wings, Trina heard the chords and pushed her way forward to watch, her tongue still huge and bubble-gum pink. Tori gave her a weak smile. Andre nodded at Tori encouragingly from behind the keyboard. The audience was staring at

her expectantly. Her brain was churning! She had to think positive. She knew the words. She knew the moves. Tori started to sway to the music; then she shut her eyes, opened her mouth, and sang.

Even though Tori was petrified, the words came out pretty, sincere, and on-key. Relaxing a little after the first few lines, Tori turned to Andre and mouthed the words *Speed it up*. He grinned and nodded to the band. They played faster as Tori found her confidence. The lights onstage flashed, turning from white to pink as the song started to build. Tori could see the two backup singers standing on a raised platform, singing and moving to the music.

Tori smiled and sang loud and strong. How could this be? She wasn't the performer in the family! But there was no time to doubt herself. There was only time to do.

Andre was standing up at his keyboard, singing along. The audience was clapping in time, tapping their feet. Tori's parents beamed. They were impressed and proud. Then the seven back-up dancers bounded onto the stage. Three girls in bright minidresses threw themselves into the routine with an electric energy while four guys leaped up the steps to where Tori stood. They lifted her into the air and carried her down to the front of the stage as she moved into the chorus.

From the wings, Trina and her giant tongue were bopping along to the beat. Even Lane was getting into it.

The dancers spread out, making a half circle on the steps behind Tori. She was in the moment and *loving* it. She knew the routine perfectly. Thanks to all the time she'd spent with her sister, she could have done it in her sleep! She'd never known performing could be such a thrill.

She finished the song, letting the last note ring around the auditorium. Then she smiled the wildest, happiest smile she had ever smiled in her life. Tori was exhilarated. The whole audience jumped to their feet.

A standing ovation? she thought. *I'm getting a standing ovation?*

The dancers hugged one another. Andre leaped over the keyboard, picked Tori up, and spun her around. Everyone who had been watching from the wings rushed onto the stage with Tori as the curtains closed. There was just one thing they all wanted her to know—she was totally amazing!

School Swap?

*WOW! Who knew singing
could give you such a BUZZ?!*

"Sweetie!" squealed Tori's mom.

"That was incredible," said her dad, giving her a massive bear hug.

"It was?" she asked, still not totally convinced by the reaction.

A man in a red shirt and black vest came rushing over. "Excuse me," he said, "but who are you?"

"I'm Tori Vega," said Tori. "Who are you?"

"This is Mr. Eikner," said Lane. "Our principal."

At once, everyone stopped talking and waited to hear what he had to say. Would he be angry that

25

a student from another school had just performed at his Showcase? Tori bit her lip, suddenly nervous.

"You don't go to school here?" Mr. Eikner asked in disbelief.

"No. I . . ." Tori didn't know what to say. She couldn't find the words to explain about Trina's tongue and the rehearsals. But Mr. Eikner had other things on his mind.

"Do you want to?" he demanded.

"Me?" said Tori in utter shock. "I don't know. Should I?" She looked at her mom and dad.

"Yes!" shouted Andre before she had a chance to say anything else.

"Yeth! Yeth!" said Trina, jumping up and down on the spot. Her tongue was still swollen, but she was obviously excited for her sister. Lane was clapping, Andre's band looked pleased, and the school nurse was smiling.

One kid was holding a ventriloquist's dummy, and even the puppet seemed to be looking at her, nodding his head.

A puppet? thought Tori. *Who carries a puppet?*

But there really wasn't time to wonder about puppets. Her whole life was changing at that very moment! Tori's mom and dad looked so proud. They had no idea that their younger daughter could sing and dance like that! It had always been Trina who pushed herself to the front, who wanted to dress up and put on shows, who was desperate to go to Hollywood Arts. But it looked like they had raised two performers, not one.

Everyone stared at Tori expectantly. They were sure she was going to say yes, but Tori was still trying to think it all through. Could she leave Sherwood High halfway through the term and start at a completely different school? She looked at the kids around her. They all looked so cool, confident, and creative. Tori didn't know if she would fit in. She wasn't used to being the center of attention like this.

"But all the kids who go here are crazy talented!" she said.

"So are you," said Andre. Tori's head started to swim.

"But what if I'm not good enough?" she asked. Why should she put herself out there just to fail? She was perfectly happy with her regular school and her mold! Suddenly, everyone seemed

to be disagreeing with her at once, and the noise and buzz of excitement was overwhelming. But Andre took control of the situation. He ran out to the side of the stage and pushed past Sinjin, the student stage manager. He found the lever that operated the curtains and pushed. The curtains swished open, revealing the backstage hubbub to an unsuspecting crowd. The audience stopped talking and stared at all the people on the stage. And everyone onstage stared at the audience. What was going on?

The school nurse gave an embarrassed little wave. The principal looked guilty. Tori's mom and dad tried to hide in the wings, but there was no way out. Then Andre strolled forward and took the stage.

"Hey!" he yelled.

"Hey, Andre!" his grandma yelled back, forgetting herself and waving—then ducking down behind her seat like a frightened rabbit.

Andre walked across the stage to the confused Tori. He grabbed her wrist and addressed the audience: "This girl doesn't know if she's good enough to go to school here." He gently led Tori to the front of the stage. "What do you people think?"

There was a huge explosion of noise as the crowd went wild. They clapped, cheered, and stamped their feet. Everyone on stage joined in.

"Okay?" asked Andre.

"Okay!" said Tori, jumping up and down and hugging Andre. She had made her choice—and a new best friend. It looked like this was only the beginning.

Chapter Seven

First-day Blues

My 1st day at Hollywood Arts.
EPIC!!!!

"See, it's just a high school!" said Trina, twirling around as she showed her sister the lockers. Her tongue was back to normal again, and she was already acting like nothing had ever happened.

It was Tori's first day at Hollywood Arts. She'd thought that after the rush from the performance had died down and she was actually at school, it wouldn't be as scary. Instead, it was terrifying. The halls were filled with students practicing dance moves, mimes, and musical performances. The lockers and walls were covered in bright, colorful street art and—was that boy wearing pajamas?

"This is *not* just a high school," protested Tori. "These kids are all artistic and creative and talented and I'm just . . . normal." She thought back to her science project with Evan. She got the feeling she wouldn't be studying much bread mold in her classes today.

"It's okay," said Trina. "There's nothing wrong with being average. Anyway, you're not alone. I've got your back!"

Tori sighed with relief. Trina was her big sister and would always be there for her. Just then, a little dynamo of a girl rushed up to them.

"Trina! Eric Paulson got his hair straightened!"

"Shut up!" Trina shouted. And off they went, leaving Tori alone. So much for big-sisterly love!

"I'm alone!" Tori said to the backs of their heads.

She looked around for someone who could help her. She saw a girl wandering down the corridor, lost in her own world. She had bright red hair and seemed friendly. Tori plucked up her courage and waved.

"Hey," started Tori. "Can you tell me—" But the girl stopped and stared at her, openmouthed.

"You're Tori, right?" she said.

Tori nodded.

"You were so awesome in the Big Showcase!" she enthused. The girl had a high, breathy voice and wide, welcoming eyes.

"Oh, thanks!" Tori said. Since Trina had bailed on her and Andre was nowhere in sight, it was good to have someone to talk to. Even if that someone was a stranger.

"My name's Cat."

"Like the animal?" Tori asked, making sure she had it right.

"What's that supposed to mean?" Cat demanded, changing from super-happy to super-upset in an instant.

"Nothing! I love cats!" Tori had no idea what she'd said wrong.

"Me too. They're so cute," said Cat, happy again. She wandered away, humming. Tori didn't call after her. Who knew what she might say wrong this time? She caught sight of a boy with a ventriloquist's dummy on his arm. She remembered see-

ing him in the wings at the Big Showcase. Maybe he would help her.

"Hey," she began.

"Hey, h-hello," he stuttered as he stopped and turned around to look at Tori. "Female," he blurted out, then looked down at the floor and then back at his dummy in panic.

Tori went on anyway. "Can you tell me where Sikowitz's classroom is?" She smiled hopefully.

"Sikowitz. Down the hall, swing left at the water fountain, second door on the right," the dummy said in a smooth voice. The boy's lips didn't even move. Tori was impressed—but wary. It wasn't every day she met a student ventriloquist.

"Thanks," she said.

"Whatever it takes, cupcake," said the puppet. The boy shrugged, implying that he had no control over what his dummy said. Tori raised her eyebrows and followed his instructions to the classroom—as quickly as she could.

Some of her classmates were already in the room, chatting and finding seats. Nervous, Tori looked around to see if she recognized any faces, but of course she didn't have any friends here.

Unless you counted the crazy girl. And the guy with the dummy. Wait, did they count as one new friend or two? Tori was lost in thought, when *THUMP!* she bumped into the boy behind her, causing him to spill his coffee all over his shirt.

"Oh my gosh!" She looked up, mortified. He had long dark hair, dreamy eyes, and a slightly surprised expression.

"It's cool," he said.

"Oh my gosh. I spilled coffee on you. Here." Tori started wiping his jacket with her sleeve as he backed away. "I think it's coming out." She continued to rub furiously, ignoring his protests.

"You might be making it worse, actually." He laughed a little.

A cute guy, she thought. *I just dumped coffee on a cute guy.*

With a cute laugh and a cute shirt and a cute smile and a cute—

"Dude!" came a stern voice from the doorway. Tori could tell it was aimed at her. She turned to see a tough-looking girl dressed in black with purple streaks in her long dark hair. She looked confident, cool, and *very* annoyed. "Why are you rubbing my boyfriend?" she demanded.

Tori tried to explain, but she was shouted down.

"Get away from him!"

"Relax," said the super-cute guy, calming his girlfriend with a kiss. Tori was amazed when the girl's expression stayed the same. A kiss from a guy like that and not even a smile?

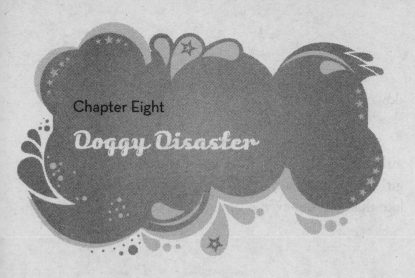

Chapter Eight
Doggy Disaster

Could today get any weirder...
or WETTER?

"Oh my god, there's a huge fire!" a voice screamed out. The classroom door swung open and a wild-haired man was standing there. He had bare feet and wore old, tattered clothes. Tori grabbed her bag, and the rest of the class leaped to their feet.

"Where?" Tori asked in alarm.

"Kidding!" said the strange man. "Kidding. Just wanted to get your blood pumping. Which I did. Ha!" He looked pleased with himself. "Now, let's get started. Rumps in chairs." Right away all the kids calmed down and sat in their seats, un-fazed, as the teacher took off his book bag and

rolled it across the floor as if it were a bowling ball. Tori looked around in confusion, saw Andre, and gratefully sank into the chair next to his.

Tori whispered, "He's our teacher?"

Andre nodded.

"Okay, first I'd like to introduce our new student, Tori," said the teacher. "And I would like to thank her for the generous gift of two dollars, which she handed me outside this morning. Not necessary, but much appreciated."

"Why did you give him two dollars?" asked Andre, leaning over to Tori.

"I thought he was homeless," Tori replied, embarrassed. But Sikowitz had already moved on.

"Today, we're going to continue our study in group improv. Tori, I assume you're familiar with improv?"

"No," Tori said, deciding it was best to come clean.

"Okay, crash course! Improv!" he bellowed. "Acting without a script. The actors must make up their own actions and dialogue as they perform the scene. Understood?"

He left no time for Tori to answer.

"Excellent," he boomed. "Jade, you will

captain the first group of the day. Choose your actors, Jade."

Jade. So that's the cute boy's girlfriend's name, Tori thought. She winced as the tough girl in the black leggings stood up, gave her an evil glare, then walked casually to the front of the classroom to pick out her actors.

"Cat," she said. The red-haired girl Tori had met earlier jumped up, looking pleased. "Beck, Eli," Jade continued. Her boyfriend and another boy stood up. Tori tried not to look at the large coffee stain on Beck's shirt. Then the unthinkable happened. "And . . . Tori," Jade finished, using a mocking voice.

Tori looked at Andre. It didn't take a psychic to see that this wasn't going to be good. But she tried to relax when she saw how much Jade was loving putting Tori on the spot. She made her way to the front of the class to join the others onstage. Then the game began.

"Let's give them a place," said Sikowitz.

"Home!" called Robbie, the boy with the dummy on his arm.

"Hoooooome!" repeated Sikowitz, but with much more dramatic flair.

"Real creative," sneered Robbie's puppet.

"You be quiet!" Robbie scolded. The dummy responded by smacking Robbie in the face.

Seeing this, Tori had to wonder, *What is wrong with everyone at this school?*

"And now we need a situation," continued Sikowitz.

"Big news!" suggested Andre.

Sikowitz frowned. "Andre, nobody wants to see big nudes," he said.

"News," repeated Andre.

"Ah well, that's different," said Sikowitz. He scrawled on the board *Home/Big News* in huge letters. Then he nodded to Jade.

"Why don't you wait in the hall?" Jade told Tori. Tori awkwardly made her way over to the door. She had the feeling something terrible was going to happen, but she had no idea what.

"Okay, at home and big news," repeated Sikowitz with excitement. "And . . . action!"

Jade started the scene.

In a voice that sounded like a sitcom house-wife's, she spoke to Beck. "Hey, babe, how was work today?" Then she put her arms around his neck.

"I got fired," said Beck, looking really sad.

"Again?" Eli piped up.

"It's okay, I have great news that will cheer up this whole family!" said Jade in her best "mom" voice. "I went to the animal shelter and got us . . . a dog!" She crossed over to the doorway, where Tori was waiting.

"Yes?" said Tori, not sure what to do. She glanced at Sikowitz, but he was drinking coconut milk though a straw. No help there. "I'm the new family dog," she said. "Uh, woof."

But Jade wasn't pleased with this. "Sikowitz, will you tell this *amateur* that dogs can't talk and that they don't walk on two legs?"

Sikowitz looked up, startled that he had been called on to help. "Sorry, I was sucking the milk out of this coconut. But yes. It's true, Tori," he said. "If you're going to play a dog, be a dog."

With a heavy heart, Tori got down on all fours and barked. Jade looked smug.

"I went to the animal shelter and got us a dog," said Jade, back in full mom mode.

Because they were playing the kids in the scene, Cat and Eli were happy about their new

pet. They got on the floor and started petting the new doggie.

"Uh-oh, it looks like this dog has bugs in her fur," said Jade, picking an imaginary bug from Tori's hair. She stepped away from Tori and wrinkled her nose. Cat, Eli, and Beck took a step back too, in character.

"Ew, gross!" Cat said in a little-girl voice.

"Woof?" said Tori. She had a bad feeling about this.

"That's okay," said Jade. "I read on the Internet that coffee gets rid of fur bugs." She walked offstage to a student in the front row and picked up his iced coffee.

"Maybe you shouldn't, um . . . ," Beck attempted, realizing exactly what Jade was about to do. But it was too late.

"Jade!" Andre shouted.

Slowly, Jade poured the drink over Tori's head. Coffee dripped down her neck and soaked her T-shirt. The rest of the class gasped in horror. Then *clunk, clunk, clunk.* Ice cubes bounced off her skull. Tori blinked to keep the coffee out of her eyes and struggled to her feet. She

stood up and was met with Jade's stony gaze.

"What's the prob . . . *dog*?" Jade asked in a malicious tone.

Tori ran out of the room as fast as she could. She'd never thought her first day could be *this* bad.

Chapter Nine
Feeling Lost

Should I STAY
or should I GO?

Tori ran down the hall and found her way back to the lockers. She was trying hard not to cry. Running her fingers through her wet, sticky hair, she plopped down on the stairs and pulled out her phone. As before, the halls at Hollywood Arts were littered with performers practicing their craft. A boy was balancing on his hands as a girl looked on. Tori was so upset that she didn't even notice them until she turned her head and found herself at eye level with the guy's backside! Tori screamed. Right about now she could have used Sikowitz to yell "Rumps in chairs!" but of course, he was back in class. Right along with Tori's pride.

Just then, Andre came out by the lockers.

"What are you doing?" he asked, as if nothing had happened.

"Calling my mom to tell her I want to go back to my old school," Tori said with determination.

"Why?" he said, looking surprised.

"Maybe because I don't like having black coffee in my hair?" said Tori.

"But I'll get you some cream and sugar and everything will be chill," Andre cooed, trying to make Tori laugh.

Tori ignored him, pressing the phone to her ear. She was wet and cranky and even Andre couldn't cheer her up right now.

"Hey, Mom?" she started. But Andre grabbed the phone out of her hand, ended the call, and shoved it in his pocket.

"Give me back my mom!" yelled Tori.

Andre shook his head. "You're going to quit this school on your first day because of one mean girl?" he asked.

Tori winced. "It's not just her. I don't fit in here with . . . all this," she said, staring around at

44

the unconventional students and colorfully decorated lockers.

"Aw, come on, it's not *that* different from other schools," said Andre. Tori looked over to see if there was still a student standing on his hands on the stairs, but he had gone.

"Oh yeah, like regular schools have improv classes with barefoot teachers or nerds with puppets or mean girls who make you bark like a dog!" she said in a rush. Just then, Robbie— the nerd with the puppet—appeared in the corridor. Great.

"Sikowitz wants you both back in class," said the puppet.

"He asked *me* to tell them!" said Robbie, glaring at the dummy on his arm.

"See?" said Tori, looking at Andre. "This doesn't happen at my old school." This was weird. Everything was weird. She couldn't stand it anymore.

"Will you guys be cool?" pleaded Andre.

"Him? Be cool?" the puppet said, then laughed hysterically.

Tori felt like a used coffee filter. She really couldn't deal with these two right now.

"You're a demon!" Robbie shouted at the dummy.

"You guys?" Tori saw a flash of red as Cat popped her head around the corner. "Sikowitz really wants everybody back in class."

"And *you* really wanted a date to prom last year, but you didn't get one!" said the sassy puppet.

"Rex!" Robbie scolded the doll.

"What's that supposed to mean?" asked Cat, looking hurt and upset. "Tell your puppet to stop being mean to me."

"Don't call him a puppet. That's an offensive term," replied Robbie. Tori looked from one student to the next in disbelief.

"Yeah! This school is pretty normal!" Tori cried in exasperation.

Andre realized he needed to calm Tori down, and Robbie and Cat really weren't helping. "Just go back to class and tell Sikowitz we'll be there in a minute," he said.

"You'd better hurry," Cat warned Tori and Andre.

"Yeah," said Rex.

"*I* was gonna say 'Yeah!'" said Robbie. Not surprisingly, Robbie and Rex continued to argue

as they walked back toward the classroom.

"Okay, this school's not normal," Andre said quickly, seeing Tori's point.

"Really?" Tori asked sarcastically.

"But *you're* not normal either. I've seen what you can do onstage. You're special. You're fantastic. You belong at this school."

Tori was touched. She still smelled like coffee, but she was touched.

Andre began to walk away but then turned back to add, "Normal's boring."

"It's true," said Cat, popping up from nowhere.

Tori sniffed, feeling a bit brighter. "That normal's boring?" she asked.

"Nooooo!" Cat wailed. "That no one asked me to the prom."

Back home, Tori couldn't figure out what to do. She washed her hair, changed her clothes, and tried to watch TV. But she couldn't concentrate. She got out her laptop and sat on the sofa, looking online for the video of the Big Showcase. It was already up on TheSlap.com, the Hollywood Arts website. She stared at the thumbnail image of

herself singing and dancing. Was that really her? She remembered the rush she'd felt when she started to sing, the electricity that had run through her veins as the audience started to clap. It was the best feeling in the world. Could she really give up the chance of ever feeling like that again?

Tori looked at the clock on the wall. She had been sitting alone for hours. School would be over for the day. All the kids from Hollywood Arts and Sherwood High would be packing up their things and going home to do math homework, memorize lines, practice scales, or learn a new verb in French. All of it took practice. Was it really that different?

She went into the kitchen to make some popcorn, then settled on the sofa and thought back over the day. How could Jade have done that to her? Tori hadn't meant to spill coffee on Beck. And she hadn't meant to rub anyone else's boyfriend. It was all just an accident. Sure, he was gorgeous, with his floppy hair and charming smile, but still, it wasn't like she was trying to make Jade jealous! She groaned as she remembered the look on Jade's face. Then she clicked play on the laptop and watched the screen—she appeared in the silver dress, dancing.

"You know, you're actually not terrible," said a voice in her ear. It was Trina. She plopped down on the sofa next to her sister and pointed at the tiny figure on the screen. "Are you really going to quit Hollywood Arts?"

"What do you think I should do?" asked Tori.

"I think you should come back," Trina said, as if it was the most obvious thing in the world. "So that I won't be known as the girl with the lame little sister who quit on her first day."

She stood up and was about to leave Tori sitting on the couch, stewing in her own juices of insecurity, when she added, "And . . . I think you were really good in the Big Showcase."

Tori was surprised. "Thanks, Trina," she said. Her sister's support meant a lot.

"But I would have been a-*maz*-ing!" Trina sang with a wink as she disappeared up the stairs.

Typical, thought Tori.

Chapter Ten

Alphabetical Improv

*Sometimes, revenge
is SWEET!*

The class watched in disbelief as Sikowitz fell through the window to the right of the classroom's whiteboard. He picked himself up from the floor, dusted himself off, and addressed the class as if his entrance had been completely normal.

"Good morning, young performers!"

"Why did you crawl in the window?" asked one student, echoing the thoughts of the rest of the class.

"BECAUSE being a performer means making interesting choices."

"That explains his wardrobe choices," joked Jade.

The door opened, and to the surprise of the entire class, in walked Tori. She had decided to give Hollywood Arts another try. She couldn't give up so quickly.

She could see the other students staring at her and whispering. Jade was fuming, but Beck seemed impressed.

"Tori! Good to see you again. Come in. By the way, have you ever thought about coming in through the window?" asked Sikowitz.

Tori shook her head and looked puzzled.

"Think about it," he said. It looked like Sikowitz was going to let the events of the previous day drop. He was a "live in the moment" kind of guy.

"Today we are going to do alphabetical improv," said Sikowitz, standing at the front of the class and throwing his arms out wide. 'What is alphabetical improv?' I hear you ask! And so I will answer.

"We give a letter to the first actor who speaks in the scene," continued the teacher. "Then the

51

actor must make his first word start with the letter. So if we start with *A,* it might go something like . . ." He snapped his fingers and pointed at Beck.

"Apples are falling out of my butt," Beck said with a sly smile.

"Lovely," said Sikowitz. "The next actor who speaks must start his line with the next letter in the alphabet—in this case, *B.* So he might say . . ."

"Bring those apples, so that we may all enjoy the fresh fruit from Beck's butt," said Andre.

"Charming," said Sikowitz. "So, who wants to lead the first group?"

Tori raised a hand. "I do," she said with confidence. She had no fear. The worst was already over. If she was going to stay at Hollywood Arts, people were going to have to learn that when push came to shove, Tori Vega was a tough cookie.

"All right, Tori," said Sikowitz. "Choose your actors."

"I choose Andre, Cat, Beck . . . and Jade." Jade looked astonished and raised an eyebrow.

"Yeah, you," said Tori.

Jade seemed shocked at the nerve of this new-

bie, but she wasn't one to back down from a challenge. She stood up and walked to where Beck stood at the front of the stage. And just to make sure everyone, including Tori, knew what was up, she gave Beck a passionate kiss.

Tori couldn't believe this girl—what was her problem?

Sikowitz wasn't happy either. "Jade, kiss your boyfriend on your own time."

"Oh, I will," replied Jade, looking pleased with herself.

"If you start your line with the wrong letter, then you are OUT," said Sikowitz. He banged his bare foot on a chair for emphasis. "Robbie, give us a letter."

"*P,*" said Rex.

"*P!*" shouted Sikowitz.

"Oh, I was gonna say *P!*" Robbie complained.

"The scene can be about anything you want," Sikowitz continued. "The first letter of the first line is *P*. Tori, action!"

"Please go and take a shower," said Tori, looking at Jade. It was not a great line, but it was a start—and a dose of Jade's own medicine!

"Quit telling me what to do," Jade replied. She

made the sentence start with the next letter in the alphabet, but it was obvious she really meant what she was saying.

"Relax, girls! Let's all try to get along," said Beck.

"Totally," agreed Cat.

"Ennnhhhh!" Sikowitz made a loud noise like a game-show buzzer. "Cat, your line had to start with an *S*."

"Oh, my life's the worst!" she cried.

Aware of Cat's easily swayed emotions, Sikowitz knew just what to do. "Here's a piece of candy," he said.

"Yay! I love candy!" Cat happily flounced back to her seat, grabbing the candy from Sikowitz along the way.

"All right, Andre. Letter *S* goes to you," he said.

Jade and Tori were glaring at each other across the stage. Andre tried to cool down the situation.

"Something bit my toe," said Andre.

"Turtle!" said Tori, diving back into the scene. "That turtle just bit his toe!"

"Unbelievable that you're even here," said Jade, refusing to get into character.

"Very immature of you to say that," scolded Beck.

"What if the turtle bite broke my toe bone?" asked Andre, trying to steer the scene back on track.

"X-rays are the only way to find out," said Tori.

"You should shut up," said Jade. She wasn't even trying to be a character in a scene. She was just being her usual crabby self!

"Zap! I healed you with my magic finger," said Beck.

"Thanks," said Andre, rubbing his toe.

"Ennnhhhh!" Sikowitz did the game-show noise again. "Andre! Your line had to start with an *A*. Sit down," said Sikowitz.

"Awww, and I just got my toe bone fixed!" Andre said as he left the stage and went back to his seat.

"Tori, letter *A* to you."

A, thought Tori. *What goes with the scene and starts with A?* Then it came to her in a flash. "Aliens!" she shouted. ". . . are the only ones who can heal toes by finger-zapping!"

"By the way . . . ," Jade began. Then she blew a raspberry at Tori.

"Correct, I am an alien!" said Beck, ignoring his girlfriend.

"Oh, a twist!" Sikowitz yelped.

"Don't hurt me, please, alien!" gasped Tori, getting into the part.

"Even though she's extremely annoying," added Jade.

"Fainting," said Beck, swaying on his feet. "Because I can't breathe your Earth's air." He collapsed onto the floor.

"Gosh, it fainted," said Tori.

Sikowitz clapped. He was enjoying himself too. "Excellent, Tori and Jade! Keep going, girls! The next letter is *H*."

But with Beck's character passed out, there was no one to stop Jade and Tori's alphabetical attack. "Hey, why don't you go jump off that cliff over there?" Jade said.

"I think *you* should," Tori countered.

"Just where did you come from?"

Tori said the first thing that came into her head. "Kangaroos!" It was a strange choice, but Tori was trying to keep up with the fast pace. That was all that mattered.

"Lousy animals, kangaroos. They're awkward and dirty."

"Maybe they learned from you?" The class was glued to Tori and Jade—this was getting nasty.

"No one talks to me like that."

"Obviously someone should."

"Please run in front of a bus!"

"Quite obnoxious of you to say."

"Really?"

"Sure was."

"Thanks."

"Up your nose I see boogers." Tori knew it was immature, but she had no time to think.

"Very clever."

"Wish you'd thought of it?"

"X marks the spot I'd like to punch," Jade replied, pointing her finger at Tori's face.

"Your finger smells weird," Tori fired back.

"Zero is what you are on a scale from one to ten."

"And back to the letter *A*," Sikowitz shouted, clearly impressed that the girls had kept going for so long.

"As if I care what you think!" screamed Tori.

"Better watch yourself!" shouted Jade.

"Can't take it?"

"Don't push me!"

"Eat your pants!"

This made Jade so angry she forgot herself for one crucial moment. "You eat *your* pants!" she screamed at Tori. Then she realized what she'd done. "Wait!" But it was too late.

"Sorry, Jade," said Sikowitz. "The next letter was—"

"*F*, I know!" screamed Jade, stamping back to her seat.

"Hey, the alien's moving," said Andre, still laughing at Jade's defeat.

"Keep the scene going!" Sikowitz said to Tori and Beck.

"Get up, alien!" said Tori, thinking fast.

"Head feels dizzy!" said Beck, getting to his feet.

"I know what will make you feel better," said Tori.

Jade looked on from her seat. Her furious expression said *She wouldn't dare!*

But Tori did dare.

"Jumping jacks?" asked Beck.

Tori shook her head and glanced at Jade before turning back toward Beck. "Kiss me," said Tori.

"Little weird. Let's do it," said Beck. He moved his head toward Tori and their lips brushed in a kiss.

Not only had Tori overcome her fear of failure, she'd kicked butt onstage *and* gotten a kiss from a cute guy!

The rest of the class cheered and clapped—except Jade. She was so angry that she stormed out of the room, slamming the door behind her.

Tori and Beck broke apart. The next letter was *M*. Tori thought for a second, then grinned.

"Man," she said. "I love this school!"

Chapter Eleven
The New Girl

Giving my new school another shot.
WISH ME LUCK!

The next Monday, Trina walked into Hollywood Arts in a pink romper and yellow platforms, talking loudly. She was completely unaware that the person she was talking to was no longer following her.

"So she said, 'You think you're better than everyone else?' So I said, 'Well, pretty much, yeah.' Which was just me being—" Trina stopped speaking suddenly, when she realized she was alone. Her younger sister had disappeared. "Tori? Come on!" she snapped at the closed door behind her.

Tori struggled through the door, wrestling with

Tori

"Man, I love this school!"

Trina

*"I got the talent,
and she got the strong teeth."*

Andre

"Normal is boring!"

Jade

"Don't push me!"

Beck

"Let's all try to get along!"

Robbie *and* Rex
"Don't call him a puppet. That's an offensive term."

Cat

"I love candy!"

Hollywood Arts

"All the kids who go here are crazy talented!"

an armful of books and bags. She looked disheveled and exhausted. It was still only her first week at Hollywood Arts. She had gotten the best of Jade, but everything was new—and a bit scary. It didn't help that her sister kept forgetting that even though *everyone* else was midway through a term, Tori was just getting started!

A folder crashed to the floor and Trina rolled her eyes at Tori, not lifting a finger to help.

"Did you *not* see me fall down in the parking lot?" Tori asked.

"It was very funny," Trina replied.

Ugh, Trina can be so condescending, thought Tori. "I wasn't trying to be *funny* . . . ," Tori began, bending down to get her folder and juggling her books from arm to arm.

But as usual, her sister wasn't listening. Trina had noticed a group of students crowding around the bulletin board in the corner of the hall.

"The new play roster!" she gasped. "Hold my coffee!" She balanced her cup of coffee on top of Tori's pile of books, then elbowed her way through the throng. Ignoring the other students' annoyed cries, she snatched the orange flyer off the wall.

Her eyes got wider as she scanned the list.

"These are so *good,*" she breathed in disbelief as she headed back to Tori, who was still trying to hold on to all her things. "Don't spill that!" snapped Trina, pointing at her coffee, still balancing on Tori's folder.

"What's so good?" asked Tori, catching the coffee cup just before it fell.

"The list of plays for the new semester." Trina couldn't believe what she was reading. "Oh my god. I am perfect for *all* of these!"

Tori craned her neck to read the list. "Is *Moonlight Magic* on there?" she asked.

"Oh yeah, number four," said Trina, not looking up. "Why?"

"Andre wrote the music for it," Tori said with a smile. "He wants me to try out for the lead."

Trina finally took her eyes off the piece of paper. "You? Why?" she asked.

Tori had had more than enough. "Take your coffee and go," she deadpanned as she handed over the cup.

"Ooh, somebody fell down on the wrong side of the parking lot," said Trina as she strutted in the direction of the canteen. Tori was relieved to see

her go. Trina had promised to help Tori settle in, but Trina was usually only concerned about Trina.

Tori's precarious pile of books and folders began to slip. Just then, Jade turned the corner.

Seeing Tori struggling, she asked, "Need some help?"

"Oh yes," gasped Tori in relief.

"Int-er-es-ting . . . ," drawled Jade as she continued down the hall.

Tori slumped. She should have known better than to expect Jade to help her. Then she heard Andre's voice. He was coming down the stairs, chatting with his friend Robbie, who had Rex on his arm as always.

"So you're saying that the film isn't scary?" Andre asked Rex. It seemed like the students of Hollywood Arts were all used to conducting conversations with a ventriloquist's dummy. They treated him like one of the gang. The whole Rex thing was weird to Tori. Even weirder: she was starting to treat Rex like one of the gang too.

"No, I'm just saying it's not as scary as tofu," Rex replied.

"Why are you always ripping on tofu?" asked Andre.

"Because it tastes like snot, and snot does not taste good!"

At that moment, Andre spotted Tori struggling to open her locker while holding all her books and bags.

"Hey, look who's here," Andre said, smiling at Tori.

"Hey, can you guys help me?" she asked. In a flash, Robbie dropped the doll so he could aid the girl he found so charming. Rex fell to the floor with a thud. Andre grinned and sauntered over to lend a hand too. Finally, Tori's unwieldy books and belongings were crammed inside her empty locker.

Robbie picked up the sprawled-out Rex off the floor.

Rex slapped Robbie in the face. Or was Robbie slapping himself?

"Ow!" Robbie protested. "I was helping Tori."

"Just get the gum off my forehead," snapped Rex. Robbie, of course, complied. When it came to Robbie and Rex, Tori could never be sure who was controlling who.

"My locker is filled. I feel complete!" Tori said.

It wasn't true. That "new girl at school" feeling wasn't going to go away so easily, but it was a start.

And saying it out loud made her feel a little better, until . . .

"Not yet!" said Andre with a smile.

"What?"

"You've got to customize it!" he said.

"Everyone at Hollywood Arts has to customize their locker," Robbie agreed.

Tori looked around the hall, taking everything in. Andre was right. How could she have missed it? The other students' lockers were an explosion of creativity—bright colors, crazy textures, cool art. Hers was gray, plain, and dull. *Wow,* Tori thought. It looked like if you wanted to fit in at Hollywood Arts, you had to really stand out.

Chapter Twelve

Psycho Sikowitz

Having a creativity crisis—
and it's not even lunchtime yet!

"What did you do for your locker?" she asked Robbie.

"I made a mosaic using all the baby bottle nipples from my childhood," he told her wistfully.

Tori couldn't hide her bewilderment, and Robbie suddenly seemed self-conscious.

"They remind me of a happier time," he said, as if everyone should know that.

Baby bottles? Tori tried to think of something to say. But it was just too strange. Instead, she asked Andre how he'd customized his locker.

"Check it out," said Andre. He led the way

past lockers displaying vases of flowers, a flamingo beach mural, and fuzzy dice.

"Follow those dreads!" Rex commanded, referring to Andre's dreadlocks.

Does the puppet have to comment on everything? Tori thought. But she didn't bother saying it out loud. She knew the answer.

Tori followed them, then gasped with surprise. Andre's locker had a keyboard stuck to the front. He grinned and played a funky beat—it really worked! A few of the students walking to class stopped and nodded in time to his tune.

It was totally hot—and totally Andre. But it didn't help Tori come up with any ideas for her locker. She needed something that reflected *her* personality. *What makes me unique?* she wondered.

Lane suddenly appeared, looking fed up. "Hey, Andre, Robbie. That squirrel is back in my office again," he said.

"I'll get the net," sighed Andre.

"And I'll get the nuts," said Robbie. For once, there was no comment from Rex.

It sounded like the squirrel made a regular appearance here. Tori was confused but also resigned—she was beginning to realize that just

about anything could happen at Hollywood Arts.

And right now she had more important things to think about than squirrels.

"I don't know what to do with my locker," she said out loud to herself. She turned back toward the only plain locker door in a very colorful row.

Her mind was still a complete blank. She'd always thought of her sister as the creative one in the family, but that would have to change if she was going to be a Hollywood Arts student.

A voice broke through her thoughts. "Do you want to see my locker?" It was Sinjin Van Cleef.

"I guess," said Tori, too polite to say no. Bad move.

"These are pieces of food that I chewed but never swallowed. I spit them out, coated them with a polyurethane resin, and stuck them on here with an industrial adhesive," Sinjin said with pride. He looked up at Tori and slowly nodded, as if thinking this *had* to impress her. To Sinjin's surprise, Tori silently turned away and sprinted down the hall. Robbie's baby bottle nipples suddenly seemed tame in comparison. *Very* tame.

Tori's last class of the morning was Theater Arts with Sikowitz, the barefoot bohemian. There was never a dull moment in this class! They were in the middle of a dramatic scene performed by Jade and Cat. Cat was holding a large, pink, soft toy pig.

"Betsy! Betsy!" exclaimed Jade in her best Southern accent. "That animal's delicious flesh can keep us *all* alive for another week."

"I don't want to be alive without Poncy," declared Cat. She was acting her heart out as she clutched the pig closer. "This pig is everything to me that my daddy never was, and I'll be—"

WHAP!

A big green rubber ball courtesy of Sikowitz smacked Cat right in the face! Cat shrieked as she toppled to the floor, pink pig and all.

"Sikowitz!" exclaimed Jade.

"What?" he said innocently.

"You hit me in the face with a ball!" Cat complained as she struggled to her feet.

"Oh, come on, a truly great actor can stay in the scene no matter what's happening around her," Sikowitz said in his thunderous voice.

His methods were unconventional even when his message was sane. Tori watched him intently.

She'd never met a teacher so smart yet so odd.

Cat touched her cheek. "But it really hurt," she protested. She looked as though she was about to cry when a loud bell rang. "Ooh, lunch, yay!" All thoughts of being hit by the ball were suddenly gone as she pranced off the stage.

That was the great thing about Cat. If you didn't like her mood, you could just wait two seconds for it to change.

"Learn your lines," Sikowitz shouted to the class. "I want everyone off book tomorrow."

In her short time at Hollywood Arts, Tori had learned the terms *improv,* which meant acting without a script, and *off book,* which meant you had memorized your entire part in a scene or play. Going off book was a lot of work, and Tori hoped she'd be able to do it.

"Hey, do you want to have lunch with us?" asked Beck.

"Sure, just let me—"

WHAP!

The rubber ball hit the wall right beside her head as she ducked just in time. She turned to Sikowitz. Sometimes it was hard to believe he was

70

an actual qualified teacher. Weren't teachers supposed to be responsible?

"What was that for? I'm not acting right now!" she said, still in shock.

"We need to chat," said the teacher.

"And 'Tori, can I see you?' wouldn't have worked?" asked Tori. She watched with regret as Beck and Andre left for lunch.

"Have fun!" said Andre on his way out.

"And don't forget to protect your face," added Beck.

Very good advice, thought Tori.

Chapter Thirteen

Ballet Boys

Andre and Robbie in TIGHTS?
That's something I have to see!

"What's up?" Tori asked Sikowitz.

"I hear you signed up to audition for a play." With his full beard, mismatched earth-toned clothes, and always-bare feet, Sikowitz seemed more like a yoga instructor than a high school teacher.

Tori tried not to look as he waggled his toes at her. "That's right. Andre wrote the music and wants me to play the lead," she said.

"You should!" announced Sikowitz.

"Yeah?" Tori was psyched.

"But you can't." He put on a sad face.

Tori didn't know what to think anymore, so she waited for Sikowitz to explain—keeping a watchful eye on the green rubber ball.

"Not until you pass . . ."—he paused dramatically, then continued—"the Bird Scene."

"The Bird Scene?" echoed Tori.

Sikowitz produced a battered script book from the desk. "Here at Hollywood Arts, every student must successfully complete the Bird Scene before they can audition for any and all school productions."

Tori took the book from Sikowitz. Why hadn't her sister warned her about this? Why hadn't anyone mentioned it? She was about to ask Sikowitz more questions when Cat popped her head in the doorway.

"Hey, Sikowitz," Cat said. "I forgot to ask you a question about the homework—"

WHAP!

Once again, Sikowitz threw the ball at her.

With a scream, Cat scurried down the hall.

"We'll never know her question!" said Sikowitz with a little smile.

Tori thought twice about asking any questions of her own. She did not want another encounter

with Sikowitz's ball. She grabbed the script book and ran.

As soon as she got out of throwing distance, Tori felt hopeful. No, her sister hadn't warned her about the Bird Scene, but one of her new buddies would help her. Life at Hollywood Arts just might work out after all.

Meanwhile, at the outdoor lunch tables, Andre, Beck, and Robbie had other things on their minds. Sitting in the sun, the guys talked about guy things, until Andre asked, "Hey, you know where I can buy a pair of ballet slippers?"

The boys were stunned. Even Rex the dummy did a double take!

"No, I don't," said Beck with a sly grin. "But I know where you can get yourself a pretty skirt and some lip gloss."

"Heh, heh," chuckled Rex on Robbie's arm. "That was a good one, Beck. Lip gloss." Robbie lifted Rex's arm in an attempt at a high five, but both Andre and Beck just glared at the dummy. Robbie shrugged and turned Rex's head away.

"Why do you need ballet slippers?" asked Beck, serious again.

"Because I signed up for ballet." Andre shrugged like it was the most natural thing in the world.

"Isn't that kind of . . . girly?" Robbie said finally.

"Yep," said Andre, a big grin spreading over his face. "Just one big room full of girls and me." Beck smiled too. *Now* he understood.

"You guys picking up what I'm putting down?" Andre asked.

"I am," said Beck, with a confident nod.

"Yeah, pretty smooth," agreed Rex.

"I don't," said Robbie.

"A lot of girls . . . who dance . . . all in one room . . . with him . . . ," Beck explained slowly.

Suddenly, Robbie got it. His face lit up as his expression changed to one of awe. Girls! A chance to meet girls. He never would have thought of that. Then he had an idea. "Would you mind if maybe I signed up too?" he asked.

"Go for it!" said Andre. He turned to Beck. "How about you, man?"

"I can't. Me and Jade already signed up for salsa dancing," he said.

"I can't eat salsa," Robbie said sadly. He was obviously thinking of a different kind of salsa.

"Why? It hurts your stomach and gives you nightmares?" asked Andre.

"No!" said Robbie, embarrassed.

"Yes!" said Rex, loudly.

"Maybe," said Robbie.

Sometimes that dummy just didn't know when to stop.

Chapter Fourteen

First Attempt

Doin' the Bird Scene today.
Nervous but READY.

The next day, Tori arrived for her theater class feeling nervous—and excited. She had spent the whole evening practicing the Bird Scene over and over at home. In fact, her mom and dad probably knew all the words by now too! She took a seat at the front of the classroom and ran through the lines one more time in her head. All she had to do was pass this test, she thought, and then she could audition for *Moonlight Magic*—and the sky was the limit!

"Drive-by acting exercise!" Sikowitz shouted from the stage. It was another day, and that meant

another crazy, shoeless outfit. This time, there were bright orange pants to complement his blue patterned sweater. "You're angry Englishmen. Go!"

"I insist you tell me who sat on my crumpet," started Robbie.

"My grandmummy went to the loo while I snogged the prime minister!" announced Jade.

"This flock of whip-poor-wills is bothering my trousers," Andre said.

"Good heavens! There's a dead cockroach in my brassiere!" shouted Cat in a loud English accent.

Even Rex got into the spirit. "Blimey!" shouted the dummy.

"I told you not to put plum sauce on my banger!" shouted Beck.

The class continued to shout out random English-sounding phrases that would surely make any actual English person's ears bleed. Then Sikowitz interrupted.

"All right, very good. Quiet down," he said, clapping his hands to get everyone's attention. Just then, Tori walked in. She was a little late and a little nervous. It was her very first acting assignment! Sure, she'd performed at the Showcase. But

for that, there hadn't been time to think. For the Bird Scene, there had been time to rehearse, but also time to fret. She felt ready, but still nervous.

"Now that we're all loosey and all goosey, the time has come for our newest student to tackle . . ." He started to stamp his feet on the floor loudly, and the rest of the class joined in. ". . . the Bird Scene! Tori, the stage is yours, although you can't take it home."

Tori gamely approached the stage. She was too nervous to appreciate just how lame Sikowitz's joke had been. If he was trying to calm her nerves, it wasn't working. All eyes were on her.

"Can I just ask a quick question before I start?" said Tori.

"Noooo," groaned Jade, throwing her head back in pure annoyance.

Tori started to ask her question anyway, but Sikowitz wasn't having it. "Just do your best. Action!"

So, in her very best prairie girl accent, Tori began.

"It was 1934 when my husband left me. Alone. Living on the prairie was a dreary existence. No telephone, no radio . . . only a large, majestic bird, with whom I shared my feelings." She glanced around at her audience. Sikowitz was sipping coconut milk straight from the coconut. Jade was looking like she had heard it all before.

"One day when I was feeling low, I said to him, 'Oh bird. You can fly. You can soar miles from this lonely place. Yet you stay. Why?'" Tori scanned the faces in front of her again. Cat was hanging on her words, Andre was smiling, and even Beck looked interested.

"And apparently, my question rang true. For that afternoon, the bird left. And so went my spirit." Tori reached the end of the scene. She had tried to show that she could act sad, strong, wistful, and brave. She hung her head to let them know she had finished, and waited. The room was silent.

Isn't it usual to get a round of applause? she thought as she slowly lifted her head. And still, no one spoke. Tori gulped. *This can't be good.*

"How was that?" she asked, looking at Sikowitz.

His answer was strange. "What do you mean?"

"Did I do the scene right?" asked Tori nervously. She bit her lip.

"Oh. No, not at all," he said nonchalantly, striding to the stage.

"So what did I do wrong?" she asked, disappointed.

"You'll have to perform the scene again tomorrow and get it right," he said as he calmly guided her from the stage and back to her chair. "Or else you can't be in Andre's play or any other."

The room was silent. No one smiled. No one moved.

"But can you tell me what I did wrong?" asked Tori desperately.

"No, I can't," said Sikowitz.

"I don't get any feedback?"

"That is correct."

She could handle the truth about her performance if someone would just tell her! As usual, she was finding being a Hollywood Arts student baffling. Nothing was ever straightforward.

Sikowitz turned to the rest of the class. "Drive-by acting exercise. You're all terrified dolphins. Go!"

He clapped his hands and all the students leaped to their feet and began making freaky dolphin noises. All the students, that is, except one.

New girl Tori Vega stood in the back of the classroom utterly confused. As her classmates flapped their arms like flippers and made strange clicks and whistles, she wondered why she had failed.

Sikowitz had moved on, and so had the rest of the class. "Live the fear!" yelled Sikowitz, pleased with his students' efforts.

Tori sat back down in her chair. *I'll just have to do more,* she thought. There was no way she was giving up that easily!

Chapter Fifteen

Whiteboard Blues

My locker's had a MAKEOVER!
But will my new friends approve?

Cat, Robbie, Rex, Beck, and Jade walked down the hall with Tori trailing behind them.

"Oh, come on! How am I supposed to do the scene right if no one will tell me what I did wrong?" she pleaded. "I thought you guys were my friends!"

"I'm not your friend," Jade reminded her. With that, she pulled Beck down the hall, and together they leaned against the vending machines.

Do they always have to be so . . . so . . . close? Tori thought.

"I was hoping we could be more than friends,"

said Robbie's dummy, leering at her. It was now clear to Tori that Robbie used Rex to say all the things he was too shy to say himself.

Cat rolled her eyes. "Yuck. It's so gross the way he's always hitting on every girl," she complained.

"I never hit on *you,*" Rex replied. He seemed to enjoy upsetting Cat.

"What's that supposed to mean?" she wailed.

"You guys!" Tori interrupted, feeling the moment slipping away from her. "*My* problem?"

"Number one rule of the Bird Scene," Beck said from the vending machines, "no one's allowed to help you."

"No one," Robbie repeated.

She wasn't going to get any clues from them.

Just then, Jade noticed something different about Tori's locker. She and Beck wandered over to take a closer look. Jade raised one eyebrow. She was definitely unimpressed.

"So *this* is what you did with your locker?" she asked.

"Yeah, you see, it's a dry-erase board with a bunch of colorful pens in a convenient cup," Tori said, gesturing to the whiteboard stuck to her locker. On the board, she'd simply written *Tori's*

Locker. Everyone crowded around as she explained her concept. "So whoever wants to can write and draw whatever they want." She tried to put on a winning smile. She felt like she was doing a TV commercial for a special new product she wanted them all to buy.

"But you're supposed to decorate it yourself," protested Beck.

"It's a Hollywood Arts tradition," added Cat.

"What's wrong with letting other people be expressive on my locker?" she demanded. She'd thought the whiteboard would be the perfect way around that particular problem. Besides, she hadn't had much time to do anything, what with rehearsing the Bird Scene, going to class, making new friends, and getting rubber balls hurled at her head.

"Well, for one thing, they can do *that,*" said Robbie. They all turned to look at the locker, where Jade was just finishing writing the first user-generated message: *STUPID.* With her addition, it now read *Tori's STUPID Locker.* She looked at them over her shoulder and made a big flourish as she placed the cap back on her pen and tucked it away—in the convenient cup. Putting her arm around Beck's waist, she gave a smug smile and walked away.

Tori's stupid locker, thought Tori. *So easy, so obvious, so . . . mean!*

"Yes?" she called after Jade. "Well, my locker's smarter than *your* locker!" She knew it wasn't the best retort, but it was all she could think of.

"How can a locker be smart?" said Cat. She frowned, trying to work out an answer for herself.

"I don't know!" Tori shouted in frustration, pulling the whiteboard off her locker. Now it was back to being just plain and gray.

She was going to have to try again. And try harder. That made two creative failures in under an hour. Was this what it meant to be an artist?

"Come on," she begged her remaining friends. "Somebody tell me how to do the Bird Scene or I'm going to cry."

"Can't," said Cat, and she walked away.

"Don't be so whiny," said Rex.

"Yeah, man up!" said Robbie.

Just then, Andre rounded the corner, ready for some ballet! "Time for our first class," he said with a twinkle in his eye.

Robbie smiled. This was going to be good! Fi-

86

nally, a place where he could hang out with lots of pretty girls. "Ooh, ballet!" he cooed, and followed Andre to dance class.

Tori slumped against her locker. It looked like she was right back to square one with both problems.

Robbie walked down the hall, slowly moving his legs as if they'd been covered in maple syrup. Now that he, Andre, and Rex were in their white shirts, black tights, and little slippers, he wasn't so sure about this plan. Andre, on the other hand, was so confident, he was on his phone, updating his status on the Slap. He wanted to make sure everyone knew what a genius he was!

"I didn't know I'd feel so awkward wearing tights," Robbie confessed.

"These things squeeze me in a *bad* way," said Rex. Robbie had dressed the dummy up in a little ballet outfit of his own.

"You won't be complaining when we're surrounded by lady ballerinas," Andre said with certainty.

They approached the room and slowly opened

the door, then stopped in their tracks. The dance studio was a large, well-lit room with a barre running down one side and mirrors on the wall. There were two high-tech speakers ready to play the ballet music. But Andre and Robbie didn't notice any of this because—to their horror—the classroom was full of *boys* in tights. Not one girl had signed up for ballet. Robbie looked at Andre and Andre looked back in dismay.

"Oh man! It's a dude ranch," said Rex in disgust. All the boys stared shamefully down at their black tights and white ballet shoes. It appeared that Andre wasn't the only guy in the school who thought taking ballet lessons was the perfect way to meet girls.

Chapter Sixteen

Round Two

So ready for the Bird Scene this time.
Gonna KILL IT.

Tori didn't get much sleep that night. She was too busy preparing for the Bird Scene. She was determined to pass this time. She would show them what she could do! She even got to class early and set up a few things.

"So, you ready?" Beck asked with a smile.

"I'm way past ready!" she answered. Rex, Robbie, and Jade gathered around Beck to hear Tori's rant. "Sikowitz wants the Bird Scene? I'm going to give him the Bird Scene. I've got props. I've got a backdrop. And to kiss up a little, I even got

Sikowitz two large coconuts." She pulled the hairy fruit from her bag.

"Those are good ones," said Beck.

"What's the deal with Sikowitz and coconuts?" asked Robbie.

"He says the milk gives him visions," said Jade.

Robbie had no time to react. The bell rang and Sikowitz grandly entered, tripping on the doorjamb. He made his way to the stage at the front of the class as if he was about to fall over, then righted himself quickly and stared around the room.

This didn't faze Tori—she was getting used to Sikowitz's oddball behavior. And his oddball choice of clothes. Today it was two kinds of plaid and tie-dye.

"We have much to do today," he announced, taking off his cross-body bag and "bowling" it to the floor as usual. "But first, Tori. The Bird Scene!"

"I'm ready," Tori said with confidence. "Before I begin, I would like you to have these two large coconuts."

She handed the coconuts to her teacher.

"Wonderful," he cooed. "You know their milk gives me visions."

"I've heard," said Tori, hoping her plan to win over the teacher was working.

"Very good!" he shouted with his usual gusto. He left the stage and joined the audience. "Everyone pay attention." He turned to Tori and gestured for her to begin.

"One sec."

She pulled on a cord at the side of the stage. With an impressive clank, a painted prairie scene unfolded behind her. A lonely farmhouse loomed against a vast orange and yellow sky. The class looked impressed.

"Ooooh, a backdrop," the teacher murmured.

Good, thought Tori. It had taken her *ages* to paint it! She took out a pair of old lady's wire-rimmed glasses and put them on. They really helped her look and feel the part.

"I'm ready."

"Delightful," Sikowitz called from the back of the class. "Action!"

"It was 1934 when my husband left me. Alone . . . ," she began. This time around, Tori felt more confident. Maybe it wasn't so bad that she hadn't passed at first. It had given her time to

prepare, and now her hard work showed.

When she got to the line "Only a large, majestic bird, with whom I shared my feelings," she turned a handle on the wall and down came a toy parrot from the ceiling, dangling on a piece of string. Her friends made approving noises.

Jade looked disgusted. The bird was a bright yellow and blue toy. Not even close to "large" or "majestic"!

"One day when I was feeling low, I said to him, 'Oh bird. You can fly!'" Tori put as much emotion into that line as possible. "'Yet you stay. Why?'" Tori looked at the toy parrot as if it were her only friend, her faithful companion, just like she had been practicing in the mirror at home. "And apparently, my question rang true, for that afternoon the bird left!"

Suddenly, she pulled a large pair of scissors from her pocket and snipped the bird's string. The toy dropped into her other hand. Sikowitz stopped drinking his coconut milk, waiting to see what his student would do next. Tori turned and chucked the toy bird as hard as she could out the window. "And so went my spirit," she ended.

She hung her head to show that she had fin-

ished, but only for a fraction of a second. She looked up at Sikowitz with an expectant grin.

"So . . . was that good?" she asked, sure the answer was yes. It *was* good—she *knew* it was. It had to be. She had put so much into it.

But Sikowitz leaned back in his chair, folding his hands behind his head. He waited a while, staring at Tori with an expression she just couldn't figure out.

"Exactly what are you asking me?" he said.

"Did you like what I did with the scene?" she asked, looking a little shaken.

"Sure!" said Sikowitz.

"So . . . did I get it right?" asked Tori, crossing her fingers behind her back.

"Oh no. You failed. Again," Sikowitz said in a strange voice.

He's enjoying this, thought Tori. Why wouldn't he tell her where she went wrong? A hundred thoughts raced through her head. Did she do the accent wrong? Should the tone of the scene have been sadder? Should she have used an eagle instead of a parrot?

She was just about to protest when a voice called from the window. "Hey!" It was the school

gardener. He was holding up the toy parrot, and he looked pretty angry. "Watch where you throw your props!" He hurled the parrot back through the window. Tori ducked just in time. That was twice in one week now that she'd had to dodge a flying object in this classroom. This sort of thing never happened at her old school.

Chapter Seventeen

No Help for Tori

Just thought of a way to find out
WHAT'S UP with the Bird Scene. . . .

It had been two days since Tori had first heard about the Bird Scene, and she still hadn't managed to get anyone to tell her how to pass the test. Things were really starting to get desperate—and desperate times called for desperate measures.

Tori spotted Cat's bright red hair at the top of the stairs by the lockers. She was hanging on the stair rail, typing a text message on her phone.

"Cat!" called Tori. "You have to try something!" She pulled out a large pair of handcuffs from her bag.

"Handcuffs?" said Cat.

95

"Uh-huh," said Tori. "Put them on one wrist."

"Okay." Cat smiled. She loved playing games!

"Now we lock the other part around here," said Tori. She attached the other handcuff to the stair railing and snapped it shut.

"Fun!" said Cat. She seemed happy with the arrangement and waited happily for Tori to do something else. Tori fished around in her pocket and took out a small bag of sweets.

"Try these!" she said.

"Ooh! Candy!" Cat took a few and stuffed them in her mouth. "Mmm . . . these are . . ." She stopped for a second. Something wasn't quite right. "These are so hot!" She spit out the candies and fanned her mouth with her free hand. "What are these?"

"Choo-Choo Peppers!" said Tori.

"They're burning my mouth!" she shrieked.

Tori knew that Cat's mouth was burning up—it was all part of her secret plan!

"I know," she said calmly. "Want some water?" She held up a bottle of water, tempting Cat to take it. Then she stepped back, holding the bottle just out of Cat's reach. Cat pulled on the handcuffs, fanning her mouth.

"Yes!" she squeaked, staring at the bottle of water.

This was Tori's moment. "Tell me the secret of the Bird Scene," she demanded in a maniacal voice, staring hard at Cat.

"I can't," yelled Cat. "And I need water!"

"Oh, fine," said Tori. She handed Cat the bottle and stamped her foot in frustration. Cat wasn't going to tell her anything, and Tori couldn't be mean for long. Cat started to gulp down the water. Tori sighed and headed to her locker. She had been sure that her plan was going to work. She was so distracted that she completely forgot about poor old Cat, who was still handcuffed to the railing.

"Wait!" called Cat, jiggling her handcuffed wrist around. But Tori didn't hear her. She went over to her locker, opened it, and threw in her books. They made a loud clang as they hit the back.

"What are you doing?" asked Beck, walking past.

"Angrily throwing books in my locker, can't you tell?" said Tori as she slammed the door shut. Beck noticed that she had put a pink horizontal

stripe across the middle. He smiled. It was even less creative than the whiteboard.

"So did you figure out how you're going to decorate it yet?" he asked casually.

"Yes, look—I put a stripe on it. Did you *see* the stripe?" Tori asked in frustration.

"I see the stripe," Beck said, unimpressed. He looked at Tori. Tori looked at the stripe.

"I don't know what to do," Tori wailed, folding her arms and slumping back against the wall. She was at the end of her rope and beginning to panic. Between the locker issue and the Bird Scene, she was totally stressed out.

"Why don't you do something creative and deep?" he said.

"What did you do for yours?" asked Tori.

"Come on, I'll show you," he said. She followed him over to his locker. He stood in front of it and gestured for Tori to stand in front of him. She waited patiently for the grand unveiling, and finally he stepped aside to reveal his locker. The metal door had been removed and replaced with a clear plastic one.

"Clear?" asked Tori. She didn't get it.

"Transparent!" said Beck, a little smugly. "I've

got no secrets, and neither does my locker."

"Aw, that *is* creative and deep," sighed Tori. Perfect for Beck. Then she remembered her other problem. "So, anyway . . . about the Bird Scene?" She thought it was worth a try, especially since she had Beck to herself for once. Jade was usually never far away from her precious Beck.

"Later!" said Beck, patting her on the head and hurrying away with a knowing grin. The bell rang for lunch and Tori groaned.

No one was going to help her. What was she going to do? She slowly walked toward the canteen, lost in thought.

At the top of the stairs, Cat wiggled her handcuffed arm in a hopeful way at the passing students. Everyone seemed to be rushing past without noticing. Then she saw Tori's sister and managed to catch her eye. "Hey, Trina! Can you help me?" she called. But Trina was running down the stairs as fast as her high-heeled shoes would let her. She was on a mission.

"Sorry, got to get to lunch before they run out of paninis!" Trina shouted over her shoulder as she rushed past, leaving Cat all alone.

Chapter Eighteen

No Escape

*Robbie and Andre want to get out of ballet—
it won't be that easy!*

Meanwhile, in ballet class, Andre, Robbie, Rex,
and the other boys stood in a group, self-conscious
in their dainty white slippers. They looked around
the dance studio uncomfortably. All twelve
guys wore identical white undershirts and black
tights.

"Man, this is humiliating," said Rex.

"Agreed. I can't believe you got us into this,"
said Robbie.

"Well, let's get *out* of this," said Andre.

The door swung open and Madame Makee,
the dance teacher, entered. With her long dark

hair swept up in an elegant bun, and wearing a flowing black skirt and leotard, she looked every bit as graceful as her class did not! Andre put on his most charming voice as he sauntered up to the Frenchwoman.

"Madame Makee," he started confidently.

"*Oui?*"

"Robbie and me, we're going to have to drop this class," he said. He put on his best sad face, but he didn't get a chance to explain himself. Madame Makee was genuinely worried.

"If you drop this class, then it goes on your permanent record as a *zero*," she said. Andre and Robbie were shocked. That would be terrible.

"Oh, come on, you can't give us a *zeh-ro*." Andre pleaded, imitating the teacher's French accent when he pronounced the word *zero*.

"Why do you want to drop this class?" demanded the teacher.

"Look around, woman!" said Rex rudely, from Robbie's arms. "We're surrounded by dudes in tights. It's just gross."

Before Madame Makee had a chance to answer, the door opened and the last student walked in the room.

"Hey, sorry I'm late," she said.

It took all the guys in the class a moment to register that the new student was a girl. Then one more moment to notice how pretty she was. She had long wavy dark hair tied up and decorated with pink flowers. She wore a pink leotard and floaty skirt. To all the boys, she was a vision of loveliness. Perhaps wearing tights wasn't so bad after all.

"Girl!" shouted Robbie, breaking the spell she had cast. Within seconds, the girl was surrounded as the whole ballet class ran to her, trying to shake her hands and say hello. As the boys approached, the girl in pink looked terrified. This wasn't how she'd imagined her ballet class would be either.

After class, Robbie and Rex—back in their own clothes—were moping by the lockers. Now they had a whole term of ballet lessons to look forward to, and eleven guys to compete with for the only girl.

Tori practically *skipped* toward them with a huge smile on her face. It was as if they were the

only people in the world she wanted to talk to. It was suspicious.

"Hi, Robbie! Hi, Rex!" she said, flicking her hair and using her sweetest voice. "Did you guys quit ballet?"

"We can't—unless we want a *zeh-ro*," said Robbie, imitating Madame Makee's French accent.

"Aww!" said Tori. She reached out and rubbed Robbie's head in a flirty way. "Well, I'm sorry you're feeling stressed."

"It's okay, I'm sure we'll . . . ," Robbie trailed off. Tori's hair-stroking distracted him. He was barely able to speak.

"Would you keep doing that, please?" he asked Tori in a stunned whisper.

"Sure," she replied.

"This is getting weird," said Rex.

"Shh!" hissed Tori at the dummy. "Hey, Robbie. You know what's making *me* stressed?"

"Tell me. I'll kill it!" said Robbie.

"It's just this whole Bird Scene thing," Tori said, as if it had only then occurred to her. She kept on petting Robbie's hair.

"There it is, the ulterior motive!" shouted Rex.

"Hush, puppet," said Tori, putting her hand over the dummy's mouth.

"Mmmm–mmmh," Rex mumbled.

Tori smiled innocently. "You'll help me with the Bird Scene, won't you?" Suddenly, she screamed, holding her hand up and shaking it. "He bit my hand!" she said in disbelief.

"Take me to the bathroom," Rex growled. "I gotta pee, *now*."

"He's a puppet! He can't pee!" yelled Tori as she watched her last hope rush off down the corridor to the boys' room.

"You don't know what I got!" Rex yelled back.

Tori was so annoyed that she swatted at Robbie's bottle-nipple locker door before storming away. This was getting ridiculous!

The next day, Robbie and Andre were back for more ballet. But with a girl in the class, Andre's attitude had changed.

With a regal air, Madame Makee gracefully swept into the room.

"All right, class!"

"All right," the boys mumbled back.

"Which dancers would like to show me the routine we were working on last time?" asked Madame Makee.

Andre's hand immediately flew into the air. "We would!" he called out.

"What?" Robbie asked, petrified.

"We got this, man," Andre said under his breath.

"You're a maniac!"

"Andre. Robbie. To the front," said Madame Makee.

Robbie placed Rex on a chair and said, "Don't talk to anyone until I get back."

Robbie then joined Andre, and the two boys assumed the starting positions for their dance. This involved standing next to each other, holding hands and twisting apart to face different directions. The rest of the class stood at the back by the barre as Madame Makee started the music.

"Begin," she cried enthusiastically.

As Robbie and Andre twirled and jumped, Andre tried to make eye contact with the new girl. With each ballet movement he did, he looked at her with a little smile, making it clear that this was *all* for her benefit. Robbie did the same, giving her a little wave whenever he was near her side of the room.

The girl smiled back politely, but she didn't seem very impressed with the general mayhem going on in front of her. Andre was not the most graceful dancer. Neither was Robbie. At one point Robbie and Andre's routine involved meeting in the middle and exuberantly slapping each other's hands. It looked more like a fight than a dance routine, and Robbie couldn't hide the pain on his face.

"Too hard," he whispered to Andre, but they couldn't stand still for long. Suddenly, they were holding hands and spinning around in a circle.

Eventually, the music swelled to a crescendo, and Andre and Robbie ran toward each other for the grand finale, leaped into the air and . . . accidentally kicked each other in the groin. Uh-oh. Groaning in pain, the friends fell to the floor. Madame Makee stopped the music.

The other boys gasped, knowing just how much that must have hurt. Even the girl in pink looked shocked.

Robbie and Andre lay on the floor, still writh-ing in pain.

"Let's take a five-minute break," Madame Ma-kee said.

"Please make it ten," said Robbie.

"Twenty," gasped Andre.

Chapter Nineteen

The Bird Scene

Ahhh! About to try the Bird Scene AGAIN—
WISH ME LUCK!

Once again, Tori arrived early to set up Sikowitz's room for the Bird Scene. She hung a large pair of floral curtains across the front of the classroom. This was her third attempt, and it had better be her last!

Andre and Robbie waddled into the room holding ice packs over their ballet injuries and wincing with every step they took. Beck and Jade looked alarmed, but before they could say anything, Sikowitz slammed the door against the wall and bounded into the classroom.

"Happy birthday!" he sang. He ran his fingers

through his beard and smiled around at the class. He was wearing the same checked trousers as the day before, but this time he had paired them with a peach and royal blue shirt. As usual, the wooden beads and bare feet finished his look.

"Whose birthday is it?" asked Cat. She must have found someone to free her from the handcuffs.

"Someone's, somewhere," said Sikowitz.

"That's so true," agreed Cat, pleased. She had never thought about it like that before. Sikowitz was so clever!

"Where's Tori?" asked Sikowitz. He hadn't noticed the curtains.

"Here," Tori piped up, poking her head through the gap in the curtains. Sikowitz jumped back in surprise.

"Ooh, you bought curtains," he said approvingly. At least, Tori hoped it was approvingly. She had put absolutely everything she had into the Bird Scene this time. She couldn't possibly fail again. Could she?

"Let's do this!" she growled through gritted teeth.

"Ladies and gentleman, once again, it's the Bird Scene! Starring Tori . . . ," Sikowitz trailed

off. It was clear he had no idea what Tori's last name was.

"Vega," she shouted, popping her head out through the curtains again.

"Vega!" Sikowitz repeated as he sat in his chair at the back of the room and picked up a coconut with a straw in it.

The curtains swished open. Tori gave her audience a moment to take in what an amazing job she'd done dressing the stage. She had added to the hand-painted backdrop of the prairie house a bare-branched tree, a tumbleweed, and a period table and chair. There was also a weather vane. For her costume, Tori wore a long dark pink skirt and apron, a gray blouse, and the glasses she had worn before. She took a remote control from her pocket and pressed a button. Gentle music filled the room. Tori looked at the expectant faces of her fellow students and began:

"It was 1934 when my husband left me. Alone." She kept her accent perfectly. She was truly committed to playing her part. When she got to the line "Only a large, majestic bird, with whom I shared my feelings," she put her fingers

to her mouth and whistled. To the amazement of the class, a white cockatoo flew through the open classroom window and landed on the weather vane by Tori's side.

Stunned, Sikowitz let the straw drop from his lips. Was he seeing things? Had he drunk too much coconut milk?

"You see the bird too, right?" he asked Beck quietly.

"Yeah," said Beck.

"Fantastic," said Sikowitz.

"One day when I was feeling low, I said to him, 'Oh bird. You can fly,'" Tori continued. Sikowitz slurped coconut milk through a straw as she spoke.

"Yet you stay. Why?" She gave a little nod to the bird, and it immediately flew out the window and was gone, just like the bird in the script.

"And so went my spirit," finished Tori. She hung her head, just as she had for the first two performances. She was hoping that someone would smile, or applaud, or do . . . something. Anything! But the room was silent, as though everyone was waiting. But for what?

Sikowitz's voice broke the quiet. "That was impressive," he said. Tori's heart leaped.

"So did I get it right?" she asked. There was a slight pause.

"Nope," said Sikowitz. Tori caught a glimpse of Jade's smug smile. That was just too much.

"But . . . you . . . I . . ." Tori was so angry that she could hardly talk. She couldn't believe she was hearing this. "I *did* get it right!" she yelled.

"Tori, listen," began Sikowitz, but Tori was so angry that she couldn't stop herself. She shouted over him.

"I'm not trying to be disrespectful, but do you know how hard I worked on this scene? I made the costume. I downloaded special prairie music. I even trained that crazy cockatoo to fly in and out of that window on command."

As she spoke, the large white bird flew in and landed on the weather vane again.

"Not *now*!" she shouted, and the bird flew back out the window. "I know you're a great acting teacher," she continued. "But I don't care what you say. The scene I just did was good. And I'm proud of it, no matter what anybody thought."

She stopped and waited for a reaction. Had she gone too far? For a moment, nobody said a thing. Then, one by one, Sikowitz and the other

students started to clap. The clapping got louder and louder.

"What?" Tori asked, confused. She removed the glasses and hung them around her neck.

"You just passed the Bird Scene!" yelled Sikowitz, punching the air.

Tori was more confused than ever. One minute she'd failed, the next minute she'd passed. What was going on here?

"But you said—"

"Tori. The whole point of the Bird Scene is to teach a performer like you to believe in their own choices no matter what others think. We are artists, and a true artist does not define success based on approval from others. A true artist need only please himself. Or herself." He glanced down at Rex sitting on Robbie's lap. "Or *it*self."

"You don't know what I got!" shouted Rex.

"So all three times I did the scene . . . ?" said Tori.

"Were delightful," Sikowitz finished, with a kind smile. "It was only wrong when you asked me if it was right." Sikowitz leaped up on the stage with Tori and clapped his hands emphatically. "All right. Drive-by acting exercise. You're all elderly people walking barefoot on broken glass. Go!"

The class jumped up enthusiastically and adopted hunched poses as they pretended to be old.

Sikowitz smiled at Tori and extended an arm. Supporting each other like a couple of old-age folks, they oohed and aahed as if walking on glass. Tori was starting to grow quite fond of her acting teacher. The relief at passing the Bird Scene was huge. She felt . . .

Well, she felt . . .

Victorious!

Chapter Twenty

Make It Shine!

Learning the lesson of the Bird Scene . . .
Now my locker has STAR QUALITY!

The Bird Scene might have been over, but there
was one more thing Tori had to do before her first
week was finished: decorate her locker door! Now,
thanks to Sikowitz's class, it didn't feel like a problem anymore. Tori was full of confidence in her
abilities. She was sure she had the most amazing
idea ever.

Tori spent the rest of the morning putting it
all together. Then she gathered everyone for the
great unveiling. She stood in front of her locker
and held the door open so that no one could peek
at what she had done. She was pleased to see all

the expectant faces. Trina, Robbie—with Rex, of course—Cat, Beck, Trina, Andre. Even Jade was there. She was staring at her cup of coffee, looking as bored as she could manage.

"You guys ready?" Tori asked in an enthusiastic voice.

"Yes," her friends said in unison.

"Whatever," muttered Jade.

With a flourish, Tori slammed her locker door shut. On the front she had painted a nighttime city skyline. Written in the middle, in funky lettering, were the words *MAKE IT SHINE.* She grinned. But her friends stared blankly back.

"Make *what* shine?" asked Trina.

"It's the title of the song I sang in the Big Showcase!" Tori explained to her sister. "Because, you know—that's what got me here in the first place?"

"I don't like it," said Jade, taking a sip of coffee from her cup.

"Maybe the words should be bigger," said Cat, trying to be helpful. She pointed to the empty space at the top of the locker, which was painted plain black.

"Yes!" said Trina, and suddenly everyone was chipping in with opinions and ideas. Tori held up

her hands and calmed them all down.

"I believe in my own choice and I don't need approval from others," she said cutely.

"Ah, the young female has learned the ways of the Bird Scene," joked Beck.

"I still think it's dull," said Jade.

"Yeah?" said Tori. She was not fazed by their reactions. She had a trick up her sleeve. "Then maybe I should . . . make it shine?"

Tori pressed a button at the bottom of the locker and the whole locker lit up with glowing stars! Tiny windows flicked on in the towers of the painted skyline and the words *MAKE IT SHINE* glowed in bright red, yellow, and green. It was really something! Anyone could see that her friends were impressed.

"Wow!" said Trina.

"Whoa!" said Beck.

"Lighty!" said Cat.

"Are we going to eat or what?" asked Jade in a bored voice.

"Oh yay, food!" said Cat, instantly distracted. Her friends turned around and made for the canteen, but Tori was happy.

"Are you coming?" asked Beck casually.

117

"Sure," said Tori. She picked up her bag, slung it over her shoulder, and followed the others to lunch. She glimpsed Andre and Robbie hobbling behind them. They were still making a big fuss over the ballet class incident, apparently.

Tori smiled. She had learned so much in just a few days. Hollywood Arts was no ordinary school, and the friends she was making were no ordinary friends.

But then, she was no ordinary girl. Yes, it looked like she was going to fit right in.